COSMIC CREATURES

A whole new world of animal rescue!

The **Friendly Firecat**

**ILLUSTRATED BY
SOPHY
WILLIAMS**

TOM HUDDLESTON

nosy
crow

First published in the UK in 2022 by Nosy Crow Ltd
The Crow's Nest, 14 Baden Place
Crosby Row, London, SE1 1YW, UK

Nosy Crow Eireann Ltd
44 Orchard Grove, Kenmare,
Co Kerry, V93 FY22, Ireland

www.nosycrow.com

ISBN: 978 1 83994 129 0

Nosy Crow and associated logos are trademarks and/or
registered trademarks of Nosy Crow Ltd

Text copyright © Tom Huddleston, 2022
Illustrations © Sophy Williams, 2022

The right of Tom Huddleston and Sophy Williams to be identified as the author
and illustrator respectively of this work has been asserted by them in accordance with the
Copyright, Designs and Patents Act 1988.

A CIP catalogue record for this book will be available from the British Library

Printed and bound in Great Britain by Clays Ltd, Elcograf S.p.A.

Papers used by Nosy Crow are made from wood grown in sustainable forests.

MIX
Paper from
responsible sources
FSC® C018072
FSC
www.fsc.org

1 3 5 7 9 10 8 6 4 2

Chapter One
The Star Eagle

From the window of the spaceship, Charlie could see the glowing blue curve of the planet's horizon. Vela was spread out below them like a patchwork quilt, its shining purple seas and crystal-blue mountains, and its endless emerald forests teeming with wildlife. Beyond the horizon, the stars shone white.

"It's almost time to land," said Random the robot, as he floated at Charlie's

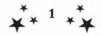

shoulder. "Take us down, pilot."

"Aye aye, sir!" Charlie saluted with a grin. She tugged on the steering stick and felt the *Star Eagle* shake and shudder around her. Gravity pushed her back into her seat.

"Is it supposed to be making that noise?" her little brother Maki piped up. He was strapped safely into the passenger seat beside Charlie, watching through the front screen as the planet rushed up towards them. The green land had given way to a great sandy desert, baked by the twin suns of Vela.

"What noise?" Charlie asked him. "I don't hear

any noise."

Maki tipped his head to listen. "A sort of rumbling. Like, *grrrrrrrr*."

"That's the engine!" Charlie laughed. "If it stops, *then* we've got a problem."

It was her tenth time flying the little landing craft, and by now she knew all the tricks. This was the first time she'd flown the *Star Eagle* without one of her parents to guide her, but Random was there to take over in an emergency.

Not that there's going to be an emergency, she reminded herself. *We're just going to have a nice quiet holiday, with no adventures.*

The sky outside turned from black to blue as the spaceship dipped lower.

Charlie could see the plain below more clearly now, with its rolling dunes and rocky gullies. It was very different from her home of First Landing, where everything was green and growing. But

★★ 3 ★★

Vela was a world of endless variety. Charlie knew she could spend her whole life exploring it and still never learn all its secrets.

"That must be the colony," Random said, and pointed to a dark blot in the distance. Peering closer, Charlie could make out the huddled shapes of buildings.

"You're right," she agreed. "I'm picking up their landing beacon. I'll let the autopilot take it from here."

She knew that even the most experienced pilots preferred to let a spaceship land itself – it was just safer that way. She swiped the screen and felt the ship's computer take control.

The *Star Eagle* swooped in, heading for a flat patch of ground with a big white circle painted on it. The engines whined and Charlie felt the soft bump

as they touched down. She unbuckled her belt as the entrance ramp began to lower. A hot breeze swept into the cockpit, bringing swirls of dry dust.

Maki unclipped his belt and joined Charlie at the top of the ramp. The second colony had only been founded a year ago, and many of the buildings were still half finished. They hunched beneath the pale-blue sky, battered by the desert wind.

"Doesn't seem a very friendly sort of place," Maki said.

"Oh, you just have to get used to it!" said a loud voice. Someone was striding across the landing pad towards them. She was short and broad, bundled into a brown jacket with a scarf across her face to keep the dust out. It made her look like a bandit, but Charlie knew that wasn't the case.

COSMIC CREATURES

"Aunt Letitia!" Maki cried, racing down the ramp. The woman scooped him up without slowing her stride. She tickled him fiercely, then she put him down and gave Charlie a warm hug. Her skin was rough and she smelled of engine oil and horse hair.

"Hello, Auntie," Charlie said. "Or do we have to call you Madam Mayor now?"

Aunt Letitia laughed. "Folks around here just call me Boss," she said with a twinkle in her eye. "Welcome to Firecat Plains, both of you. I know it doesn't look like much, but I couldn't wish for a better home. The skies are wide, the suns are warm and the earth is full of useful metals and minerals!"

"We can't wait to look around. Can we,

Maki?" She nudged her brother.

"Um, sure," he managed.

"Well actually, that'll have to wait," Aunt Letitia said, striding past them up the ramp. "I just got word this morning. They're on the move."

Charlie followed her aunt back into the *Star Eagle*'s cockpit, watching as she strapped herself into the pilot's chair and began to flip switches.

"What's on the move?" Charlie asked, confused.

Aunt Letitia pulled her scarf aside and gave an excited grin.

"The reason I invited you both out here," she said. "But I don't want to spoil the surprise. Come on, buckle up."

Charlie and Maki did as they were told, and Random bobbed between them as the *Star Eagle* took to the air again. Charlie gazed at the town of Firecat Plains spread out below.

"What's a firecat?" she wondered aloud. "Why is the town called that?"

But her aunt just smiled again and gave a mysterious wink.

Aunt Letitia flew the *Star Eagle* across the plain towards a range of rocky mountains. "You got here just in time," she said. "This only happens twice a year, and it really is an unmissable sight."

She twisted the stick, aiming for a patch of flat ground at the base of a tall cliff. On either side of it, narrow canyons cut deep into the rock.

"Those are the Ragged Ravines," she explained. "The only clear route through the Umber Mountains."

Charlie felt the landing legs touch down and smelled the hot wind as the ramp lowered. Aunt Letitia strode down, and Maki raced after her. Charlie looked at

Random and shrugged, then they both
followed.

Before them the mountains rose tall and
bare. In their shadow sat the *Star Eagle*, the
dust of the desert already coating her steel
hull.

But that was odd – the spaceship appeared
to be trembling. Had Aunt Letitia forgotten
to turn the engine off?

Then Charlie realised. The ground was shaking.

She could feel it through her boots. There was a sound too, growing louder. A low, drumming rumble, like the pounding of many feet.

"Here they come!" Aunt Letitia said, squeezing Charlie's arm excitedly and

pointing towards the mouth of one of the canyons.

At first, all Charlie could see inside the ravine was a faint blue glow, like an approaching dawn. But it was already daytime – and the glow was growing brighter.

Suddenly something burst from the canyon's mouth. For a moment Charlie thought it was water: a great river gushing from the ravine.

Then she saw paws pounding the earth, causing clouds of dust to rise. She saw blazing yellow eyes and sleek electric-blue bodies.

"They're animals!" she cried out. "A whole herd of animals."

Her aunt beamed. "Those, my dear, are firecats."

Chapter Two

The Great Migration

The firecats flowed from the Ragged
Ravines and out on to the desert plain.
They swept past the *Star Eagle* on both
sides. The noise they made was deafening.

There must be hundreds of them, Charlie
thought, *or even thousands.*

The pack moved in such close
formation that they seemed like a single
creature, with a single mind. It was only
when she squinted that Charlie could

make out individual animals.

They reminded her of the cheetahs she'd seen in old clips from Earth, but their fur was a vivid blue and these creatures were far faster. Their legs pounded powerfully as they passed like a raging torrent on either side.

Charlie felt a thrill of excitement as the ground shook beneath her. Maki squealed with joy, and even Random let out a beep of pleasure.

"I try not to miss a single migration," Aunt Letitia said. "They run all the way from the far side of the Umber Mountains to the Paradise Coast, six hundred miles away. And it's all in search of food."

"What do they eat?" Maki asked, a little nervously.

"Not little boys," Aunt Letitia chuckled. "Small mammals and fish, mostly. You should see them swim; it's almost as beautiful as watching them run."

The firecats had cleared the canyons now, leaving a trail of paw prints and stirred-up sand. The dust rose in a great plume behind them. Slowly, the trembling in the earth began to fade.

Charlie felt her heartbeat slow. "That was amazing," she said. "Thanks, Aunt Letitia."

Her aunt beamed. "It was my pleasure. I know how you've always loved animals."

"I just have one question, though," Charlie added.

"Why are they called firecats?" Aunt Letitia grinned, before Charlie could ask. "I knew you'd want to know. Well, the thing is—"

Suddenly she broke off, frowning. Charlie could feel it too – the ground was shaking again, the sound of running paws getting closer. Soon the earth was trembling so violently that Charlie almost lost her balance.

"What's happening?" she shouted over the rising din. She could see nothing but shadows through the clouds of dust.

"I don't know," her aunt said. "This has never happened before."

"I saw something!" Maki said, pointing. "Something silver, over there."

He pointed across the plain but the dust

was too dense.

"Another ship?" Aunt Letitia asked.

Maki shrugged. "I didn't see it clearly."

Then the clouds lifted and Charlie saw the herd of firecats hurtling back towards them. But they weren't moving gracefully as they had before. Now they were like stampeding cattle, shoving against each other as they ran.

"This isn't normal. Something's scared them," Aunt Letitia said. "Quick, back to

the ship!"

Charlie grabbed Maki's hand, pulling him with her. Random floated behind, throwing up a force field to protect them. Charlie looked back and saw an advancing tidal wave of fur and flashing eyes.

They sprinted up the ramp into the *Star Eagle* and Random closed the hatch behind them. But before Charlie could breathe a sigh of relief there was a sudden, dreadful crash, right above their heads. It was followed by another, as though something heavy had landed on top of the ship.

"They've started an avalanche!" Aunt Letitia shouted above the noise of more rocks tumbling down the cliff and crashing on to the roof. The ship's steel hull was one metre thick and designed for outer space, so Charlie knew they'd be safe, but the sound was still alarming.

She gripped Maki's hand, feeling him

wince at every crash and thump, until the noise began to fade. The avalanche petered out. The ground stopped shaking and soon the silence returned.

"Let's get out of here," Aunt Letitia said, turning to the *Star Eagle's* control panel. But when she tapped the screen, nothing happened. The computers were dead and the engine was silent.

Random plugged himself into a socket on the wall, tipping his metal head as though listening. "I'm afraid the main power is out," he said. "And the radio too."

"So we can't call someone to come and get us," Charlie realised.

"Firecat Plains is too far to walk," Aunt Letitia said. "It would take all day and night, and the heat out here can be intense."

Charlie frowned. "Maki, how sure are you that you saw a ship?"

Her brother shook his head. "Not very

sure. I think I did, but..."

"It wouldn't be one of ours," Aunt Letitia put in. "We only have one small loading craft, and it's black, not silver. Also, our people don't come out this way very often. Which also means it could be days before they find us."

"And we only packed enough food for a short flight," Charlie remembered.

"I can travel faster than a human can walk," Random said. "At top speed I calculate that I could reach the town before nightfall. If my batteries hold out."

"But what if they don't?" Charlie asked worriedly. "I should come along. You can carry me with your force field. That way, if your batteries do run down, I can still walk the rest of the way to Firecat Plains."

"I don't like it," Aunt Letitia said. "You'd be out in the desert, with night coming in."

"I'll have my mini-com," Charlie said,

holding up the little communication device. "I can stay in touch with you until we're out of range, then when I get closer, I can contact someone in town."

Aunt Letitia considered this, then she shook her head. "I should go. You and Maki stay here, where it's safe."

At this, Random made an uncomfortable noise. "The truth is," he said awkwardly, "over long distances my energy field is only powerful enough to support myself and one other object. An object that weighs less than—"

"I get it," Aunt Letitia interrupted with a chuckle. "I'm too heavy."

"Any adult would be," Random said quickly. "Charlie is just small enough."

"I could go," Maki said. "I'm even lighter."

But Aunt Letitia shook her head firmly. "Not on your life, little one."

"We'll be really careful," Charlie promised

COSMIC CREATURES

her aunt. "And we'll stay in touch as long as
we can."

"I will not allow any harm to come to
her," Random promised.

Aunt Letitia sighed. "Very well. But take
as much food and water as you can safely

carry. And don't tell your parents."

They used the manual controls to lower the ramp, stepping down on to the desert plain. Random extended his force field and Charlie felt the familiar prickly sensation as it wrapped around her. Her feet lifted

gently off the ground.

"My energy field will have the added benefit of protecting you from the suns," Random said.

"Great," Charlie said. "So at least I won't get burned to a crisp!"

She waved to Maki and her aunt as Random picked up speed, carrying her out across the plain. Below her floating feet, she could see the scars left by the firecat stampede. There were countless claw marks and paw prints, and tufts of drifting fur.

Then Charlie saw something moving up ahead.

"What's that?" she asked Random. "Over there."

The robot narrowed his electronic eyes, scanning the dunes. "A creature of some sort. But I don't think it can be one of those cats. It's too small and it's moving very slowly."

"We should take a look," Charlie said. "I know it's not our mission. But it's not far away."

"Very well," Random agreed.

He sped towards the shape, and as they drew closer Charlie saw that the robot was wrong. It *was* a firecat.

Or rather, it was a firekitten, a furry blue bundle dragging itself across the stony plain. It let out a mournful mew, and Charlie felt her heart sink.

"The poor thing must've got hurt in the stampede," she said. "Random, put me down. We have to help!"

Chapter Three
The Firekitten

The electric tingle of Random's force field retreated and Charlie felt her feet gently touching the ground. She hurried to the wounded creature and knelt beside it in the dust.

The firekitten's fur was paler than her adult relatives. Up close Charlie could see that the creature had faint reddish stripes too, almost buried in the blue. She reached out and picked the kitten up

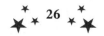

gingerly, whispering to keep her calm.

"There now," she said, stroking the trembling creature. "Don't worry, I'm a friend."

The firekitten let out a soft, helpless mew, but she didn't try to wriggle free. Very carefully, Charlie took hold of her injured paw and spread the little pink pads for a better look. Right away, she saw the problem.

A small sharp stone was wedged between the pads. Charlie probed the paw with a cautious finger, but the firekitten started to protest so she drew her hand back.

"It's wedged too deep," she told Random. "I can't get it out without hurting her. We'll just have to take her with us. Hopefully someone in Firecat Plains will have a pair of tweezers."

The kitten mewled and peered up

at Charlie. Just then a sunbeam broke through the dust cloud and shone in her yellow eyes, making them glow like the twin suns of Vela in a clear-blue sky.

"Sunlight," Charlie decided. "That's what I'm going to call you." She stroked the firekitten's fur and the little creature purred warmly.

Then Charlie tucked the kitten under her jacket. "Come on, Random. Let's get moving."

They continued across the desert, heading towards a rocky ridge some distance away. "Look," Random said, pointing with a metal arm. "That plume of dust."

Charlie could see it too, rising beyond the ridge. "It must be the firecat herd," she said. "It's too dark to be dust though. It looks like smoke."

Even at top speed, it took Random

more than an hour to reach the top of the ridge. By now they could clearly make out a solid column of black smoke rising into the pale sky.

Charlie asked Random to put her down, and climbed to the peak of the ridge. She crouched and peered over the edge. Sunlight poked her head out from Charlie's jacket and licked her face, but Charlie barely noticed. She was too distracted by what she could see in the rocky valley down below.

It *was* a spaceship, and not just a little lander like the *Star Eagle*. It was shaped like a huge flat saucer, with curved steel sides and the words *Silver Streak* painted on the hull. This ship was made to travel the huge distances between the stars, with room for at least ten people and a faster-than-light engine coughing black fumes.

Charlie could see the crew now, bustling

around the bottom of the main ramp.
Off-worlders were a rare sight on Vela.
The planet took so long to reach that, for
most space travellers, it wasn't worth the
effort. So why had they come?

A man strode down the ramp. He had
a round head and broad shoulders, and

was clearly the leader. He pointed at
something on the ground and two of the
crew went to pick it up.

As they raised it, Charlie saw the shape
clearly. Her stomach rolled over.

It was a firecat, but its head and legs
were limp as if it were asleep.

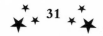

COSMIC CREATURES

"It's been stunned," Charlie said to Random. Last year her parents had had to do the same to their mooncalf, Luna, after she got her front hoof stuck in a furbit hole. It didn't hurt the animal but meant it could be handled easily.

"It's not alone," the robot replied. "Look."

Following his metal finger, Charlie spotted two more firecats in a steel pen near the ship. These were awake, prowling restlessly, butting at the walls but finding no way out. Charlie was horrified to see the proud creatures trapped in a cage.

"These people must be rustlers!" she realised. "They're stealing the firecats. But why?"

"For a zoo, perhaps," Random said. "Or a collector back on Earth."

Suddenly Sunlight let out a yowl, struggling inside Charlie's jacket.

"You're safe," she whispered. "I won't let

them get you."

But then she heard a louder cry, an
angry roar echoing from below. One of the
firecats in the pen was looking up towards
them, pawing frantically at the fence.

One of the rustlers glanced up, and
Charlie ducked hurriedly behind a rock.

"That must be Sunlight's mother," she
realised. "We can't let them take her away
on their ship. We have to stop them, or at

least chase them off."

Random's eyes opened wide. "That sounds dangerous. Your aunt wouldn't like it. She sent us to find help, not drive off rustlers."

"But we can't just leave those poor cats," Charlie insisted.

Random gave an electronic sigh. "Very well," he said. "I have an idea. But, Charlie, I insist that you stay here. It might be dangerous."

Charlie was about to protest, but deep down she knew he was right. She looked around, spotting a low-roofed cave in the rocks a short distance away.

"I'll wait for you in there," she said. "And I'll keep out of sight."

Random nodded and floated away, staying low to the ground. Charlie ran to the cave and ducked inside. It was bigger than it looked, snaking deep into the hillside. But she stayed by the entrance, looking down the slope to where the rustlers were carrying another firecat towards their ship.

"Don't worry, Sunlight," she whispered to the kitten. "We'll rescue your family."

"And just how do you expect to do that?" a voice demanded. Charlie whirled round.

A shape was approaching from the back of the cave. Charlie squinted, but she couldn't make it out clearly.

"Who are you?" the figure asked. "Why are you spying?"

Charlie backed up against the wall. "I'm not spying. Those people are stealing wild animals."

The figure floated into the light and Charlie saw that it was a boy not much older than her. He had spiky

★★ 35 ★★

brown hair and a grey uniform with *Silver Streak* printed on the breast. He was standing on a hoverboard, but as he drew closer he hopped down and faced Charlie.

"It's not stealing if they don't belong to anyone," he said with a sneer.

"The firecats belong to themselves!" Charlie said. "You can't just take them."

"And who's going to stop us?" the boy asked. "You?"

He folded his board and put it in a large rucksack on his back. Then he strode past Charlie to the mouth of the cave. "Mum!" he shouted. "Mum, I found a—"

A sudden, terrible noise made him stop in his tracks.

It echoed from the walls of the narrow valley – a deep, rumbling roar that seemed to come from everywhere at once. It was followed by a series of loud thuds, like the crashing footsteps of a huge and dreadful beast.

The boy froze, his hands trembling. The rustlers broke off from their work, looking around fearfully. Charlie grinned and clutched Sunlight tighter.

Chapter Four

Tweezers

The roar sounded again, growing louder as if the terrible creature was coming closer. The boy let out a whimper and ran from the cave, scrambling down the steep slope towards the rustlers' ship.

But he was too late.

Charlie saw the rustlers dashing towards the ramp. To her dismay they were carrying the last firecat between them. They hurried in and the ramp closed. Then the engines spat fire and the *Silver Streak* took off and vanished into the blue sky.

The boy stood open-mouthed at the foot of the slope. Charlie skidded down beside him. "They left you behind!" she panted.

"They didn't know I was out here," the boy said. "I told my mum I was going to my room to study star charts, then I sneaked out to have a look at that cave."

He looked around fearfully. "The monster. We should get under cover!"

But Charlie shook her head. "It was just a trick. Look, here's the dreadful creature that made it."

Random roared one last time as he came floating towards them. He had a satisfied gleam in his electronic eyes.

He stopped when he saw the boy. "Charlie? Who is your friend?"

The young rustler frowned. "We're not friends. My name's Taika, and that was my ship you just chased off."

Random bobbed in place. "My name is Random," he said. "And this is Charlie."

"And this little ball of fur is Sunlight," Charlie said, opening her jacket. "It's her family your people just kidnapped."

The wounded firekitten peered out. Her eyes were wide and she was quivering.

Taika's mouth dropped open. "A young firecat!" he said. "We were hoping to capture one. They'd be worth fifty of the full-grown cats."

Charlie shielded Sunlight. "Well, you can't have her, for any price. Honestly, is that really what you do? Fly to different planets and steal animals?"

Taika blushed. "Everyone's got to make a living."

"It's awful," Charlie said. "And I bet it was

your ship that started the stampede that
got Sunlight injured."

She held up the firekitten's wounded paw.

Taika squinted closer.

"It's just a little stone," he said. "I've got some stuff in my pack that'll take care of it. I've looked after plenty of animals. It's part of the job."

Charlie looked at him suspiciously. "Why should I trust you?"

Taika shrugged. "It's up to you. But I've got antiseptic and a bottle of water in my pack too. We can clean her paw properly once we've taken out that stone."

As the suns sank, Charlie stood in the mouth of the cave, talking to Aunt Letitia through her mini-com. It was only designed to work over short distances so the signal was very crackly.

"Me and Maki are working to repair the *Star Eagle*," Aunt Letitia said. "He knows even more about computers than I do. Your mother trained him well!"

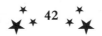

Charlie laughed. Maki had a knack with computers the way she had a knack with animals.

"We're going to take shelter in this cave overnight," she told her aunt. "Then in the morning me and Random can carry on to Firecat Plains and fetch help. He's worried about his batteries lasting that long, but we should be OK."

"And I suppose you'll have to take this boy with you," her aunt said doubtfully.

"We can't just leave him out here," said Charlie. "Anyway, I don't think he means us any harm."

"And what if the rest of the rustlers show up?" Aunt Letitia asked.

Charlie frowned. "Don't worry, Random is with me. And we'll be extra careful, I promise."

"Make sure you are," Aunt Letitia said. "Over and out."

Charlie stood for a moment,
watching the desert sky turn purple
and gold. Then she heard her name
being called and stepped back into the
cave.

"The antiseptic is ready," Taika told
her. "And I've put some soothing cream
on Sunlight's paw so it shouldn't hurt
too much. Here, you hold her still

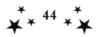

while I take the stone out." He held up
a pair of tweezers.

Random increased the light from
his silver eyes so they shone like torch
beams. Charlie took hold of Sunlight,
stroking the kitten's head to keep her
calm. She held the wounded paw and
very gently turned it over.

Taika leaned in with his tweezers.

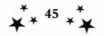

"There, now," he said soothingly. "It won't hurt a bit, I promise."

Sunlight wriggled as he seized hold of the stone and drew it out from between her soft paw pads. Charlie held on to the little firekitten, nuzzling her fur as Sunlight whimpered.

Taika tossed away the stone, then he took a soft cloth and dipped it in the antiseptic. He gently cleaned Sunlight's paw, then patted her on the head and smiled. "All done."

Charlie inspected Sunlight's paw as the firekitten licked her hand. Then the little furry creature wriggled towards Taika. Sunlight nuzzled against his arm and he looked down in surprise. The firekitten purred and Charlie watched, wondering. Taika might be from a family of rustlers but was he really as bad as he seemed?

"You don't need to thank me, little firecat," the boy said, tickling Sunlight behind her ear. Then he looked up at Charlie. "You know, I've been wondering. Where did they get that name? It seems a funny thing to call a creature that's bright blue. Surely watery-cat would make more sense."

Charlie laughed. "I'm not sure. She's got these reddish stripes, but they're really faint. I was just about to ask my aunt about it when you started that stampede."

Just remembering it made her feel annoyed all over again.

Taika frowned. "I can see you don't approve of us. Our way of life must seem strange to you."

"It's not strange, it's wrong," Charlie said. "I bet it's illegal too. When we get to Firecat Plains I'm going to have them track down your ship and free those cats. I wouldn't be surprised if my aunt decides to lock your people up."

Taika flushed angrily. "You don't get it, do you?" he asked bitterly. "We don't all have nice comfortable planets to live on. The galaxy can be a pretty tough place.

But you obviously don't know anything about that."

And he lay down with his back to her, stuffing his jacket under his head.

Charlie felt a twinge of guilt. She knew that Taika had a point. She'd travelled from Earth to Vela when she was just a little girl, and she hadn't left the planet since. This beautiful, peaceful place was all she really knew.

She lay on her coat, hearing Random humming nearby and Sunlight softly purring at her side. The wind whistled around the cave, and these gentle sounds soon lulled her into a deep sleep.

Chapter Five
Shifting Sands

They set off bright and early the next morning. Taika floated on his hoverboard beside Random, who carried Charlie in his force field.

Charlie held Sunlight close against her as they left the rocky foothills and struck out across the desert. The firekitten's paw seemed to be healing already, and Sunlight purred happily as they picked up speed.

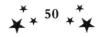

She loves travelling fast, Charlie realised. *It's in her nature.*

Sand dunes rolled like waves ahead of them, and even through the force field Charlie could feel the heat of the rising suns. She wondered how long it would take to reach Firecat Plains. Hopefully they'd be there long before nightfall.

In the far distance she spotted a haze of dust rising into the sky. Sunlight saw it too and let out an excited meow.

"It must be the firecat pack," Charlie told Random. "When we've rescued Maki and my aunt, we can take Sunlight back to them. Then we can track down those rustlers."

The robot nodded. "That would be

a fine kettle of fish, Mr Charlton."

Charlie looked at him in surprise. "Um, what did you say?"

Random tipped his metal head. "I said, those antelopes are a delightful shade of twilight, Madam President."

Looking down, Charlie realised that the

robot's pace had started to slow. Taika had pulled ahead but now he looked back, and Charlie waved.

"Hang on! Something's wrong."

The boy slowed, hopped down from his hoverboard and put it in his backpack. Random's force field lost power without warning and Charlie gave a yelp of surprise as she dropped to the ground. Sunlight scrabbled beneath her jacket so she took the little firekitten out and placed her on the sand.

Random floated forward a little way then he too slowly sank into the dust.

"Is it your batteries?" Charlie asked, crouching at his side.

Random nodded. The gleam in his eyes was flickering like a faulty light bulb. "You win the big prize," he said, his voice getting deeper as it slowed. "Three cans of beetle soup and a sock full of ... full of..."

He fell silent and the light in his eyes blinked out. Charlie sighed and patted his metal dome. The robot would be fine once they got him to a power socket, but until then they were stuck in the middle of nowhere.

"What are we supposed to do?" she wondered aloud. "I know which way to go, but I'm not sure how far it is."

She reached out to stroke Sunlight's head, but to her surprise there was nothing there. She looked around, then she heard a plaintive mew.

Charlie jumped to her feet. While she'd been distracted with Random, Sunlight had decided to go exploring. Now she was sitting on the sand some distance away, yowling in distress.

Suddenly Charlie realised.

Sunlight wasn't sitting on the sand.

She was sinking into it!

"Taika!" Charlie gestured frantically to the boy, who was closer to the kitten than she was. "Sunlight's in trouble. Help her!"

Taika saw right away what was happening. He dropped his backpack, hurrying across the sand towards the firekitten. He bent down, scooped Sunlight up in his arms and turned back.

But when he tried to lift his leg, it wouldn't come. He struggled, but that only made him sink deeper.

"I'm stuck!" he cried out. "The sand's pulling me down!"

Charlie frowned. She should've thought of that.

Taika was up to his knees already. He flailed with his arms, trying to pull himself up, but he just ended up with fistfuls of sand.

Charlie looked around. "Where's your hover thing?"

"In my pack," Taika said, pointing. Charlie saw his backpack nearby, but it too was sinking rapidly. As she watched, it vanished into the sand.

"My mum's going to kill me!" Taika moaned. "She saved up for months to buy that board."

"That won't be a problem if you keep sinking," Charlie reminded him.

He was up to his waist now, looking at her desperately. Sunlight was perched on

his shoulder, and as Charlie watched she started licking his face. Taika groaned.

Charlie forced herself not to laugh. "Sunlight's just trying to help."

She began to move closer, testing every step carefully. The sand was firm at first, but then she felt it soften beneath her boots.

"This is as far as I can go," she told Taika. "Hang on."

She peeled off her coat and sweater and

tied the sleeves together as tight as she could. Taika had sunk up to his chest now, spluttering as Sunlight tickled his face with her whiskers.

Charlie leaned out as far as she dared then she flung the bundle of clothes, keeping hold of one of the sleeves. It fell just out of reach of Taika's flailing arm.

"Try again!" he called out.

Charlie gathered the bundle back in and threw it again. This time it fell right next to his hand and Taika took hold. Sunlight meowed excitedly, hopping on to Taika's head and weaving her tail like she was about to pounce on Charlie's jacket.

Charlie stepped back to safe ground then she dug her feet in and began to pull as hard as she could. The cloth strained, and so did her arms, but slowly Taika began to slide towards her, pulling free of the sucking sand.

"It's working!" he shouted, as Sunlight ran happily up and down his back. "Keep pulling!"

Charlie gave another tug, seeing his legs kicking free. By the time he was safe on solid ground, she was exhausted. She lay back on the warm sand, panting.

Taika flopped down beside her. "You... You saved my life," he said, sounding almost surprised.

"Not just me," Charlie said, as a soft head nuzzled her neck. "Sunlight helped, remember?"

They both started to laugh in relief, lying sprawled on the sand as the firekitten bounded over them, hopping from Taika to Charlie and purring. Charlie had no idea where they were or how they were going to get help, but for a moment she was laughing too much to care.

Then, without warning, there was a
loud rushing noise, and they both sat up.

A saucer-like shape streaked across the
sky. As it drew closer Charlie recognised
the *Silver Streak*. Its thrusters hissed as it
came in to land.

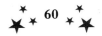

Chapter Six
In the Brig

The *Silver Streak*'s captain marched
Charlie aboard the ship, leading her
through a large open hangar and into a
long metal corridor.

"You'll be quite comfortable in the
ship's brig," he said, stopping at an open
door. "Until we can decide what to do
with you."

He was tall and stern-faced, and the
badge on his uniform read MAJOR

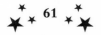

KOTO. Charlie didn't argue. She stepped into the small prison room. It contained only a bed and a sink.

Another rustler rolled Random in behind her, propping the motionless robot against the wall. Random's metal arms hung limp at his sides and his eyes were closed.

"Don't think about trying any tricks," Major Koto told Charlie, waving a finger in her face. "Your robot friend may have fooled us with all that ridiculous roaring, but now you're our prisoners, and you won't fool us again."

It was Taika who'd revealed the truth about the fake monster, and Charlie was still annoyed about it. Now the boy stood nearby with a guilty look on his face, beside a weary-looking woman that Charlie assumed was his mother. She wore a pilot's flight suit, with an image of the *Silver Streak* stitched to the breast.

Then Charlie felt a soft tickling under her jacket and remembered that there was one secret Taika hadn't revealed – at least, not yet. She crossed her arms over her chest as the major loomed over her.

"Please, just take me and Random to Firecat Plains," she said. "We won't say anything, I promise."

But the captain shook his head. "Not until we're finished with those firecats. Our hold was only half full when you

frightened us off. We're going to find that herd and grab as many as we can, then I'll think about returning you to your people."

Charlie looked at Taika but he lowered his head, unable to meet her eye.

"Aren't you going to say anything?" she demanded. "Are you just going to let him steal those poor creatures and keep me locked up, after I saved your life and everything?"

Taika opened his mouth, but before he could speak his mother took hold of his arm. "Come on, son," she said. "Let's leave this troublemaker alone, shall we?"

Taika let her lead him away. Major Koto chuckled. "You see? No one's going to help you. So just keep quiet and stay put."

He pressed a button and the door slid shut. Charlie heard it lock fast.

She sat on the bed and took Sunlight from her jacket. She gently stroked the little blue kitten. "We're in a fix now," she said. "Even if they do let me go, they're still going to try and steal the rest of your herd. We have to do something."

Charlie spotted a power socket on the wall and rolled Random towards it. She unravelled the charging cable from his side and plugged it in. She saw a flicker in his eyes but she knew it would take a while for him to come back online. Random was an old droid and his systems were rusty. But he was still Charlie's best friend.

"Maybe when he wakes up he'll know how to get us out of here," she said to Sunlight, and the firekitten replied with a soft mew.

To Charlie's surprise, it was answered by a distant, echoing rumble.

Sunlight's ears pricked. Charlie got to her feet, looking around. High on the wall was a small metal grate, covering what looked like an air duct.

"Make that noise again!" she told Sunlight, holding the kitten up. "Go on!"

Sunlight let out an inquisitive meow, and again Charlie heard a low, far-off purr — more than one, in fact. "It's the other firecats!" she said. "This vent must connect to where they're locked up. Come on, let's have a look!"

She propped Random beneath the grate, apologising as she balanced unsteadily on top of his round head. She gripped the grate and with a hard tug the entire panel came loose. Beyond it was a dark tunnel, just big enough for Charlie to climb into.

She popped Sunlight in first then clambered up, kicking and struggling as

she squeezed into the ventilation shaft.
Cool air tickled her skin, and through
the walls she could hear the rumble of
machinery. Then Sunlight mewed again
and Charlie heard the low growling up
ahead.

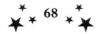

"Lead the way," Charlie told the firekitten. "Take us to your pack."

Sunlight bounded ahead excitedly, her paws skittering on the smooth metal surface. Charlie struggled to follow, scrabbling on her hands and knees.

But the air duct turned left and right, and soon Sunlight had vanished from view. Charlie paused, trying to get her bearings.

She could feel a breeze on her face and, reaching with her arms, she realised she was at a junction where three ducts met. But it was so dark, she couldn't even see her fingers in front of her face. Which way was she supposed to go?

"Sunlight!" she called, listening for the patter of the kitten's paws. She couldn't hear anything, just the rattle of the ship's engines. "Sunlight, where are you?"

Suddenly she blinked. There was light

up ahead, and it was growing brighter. It was a deep flickering orange colour, like a bonfire in the distance. It shone from the left-hand air duct, and finally Charlie heard feet scampering towards her.

Sunlight bounded from the tunnel, running up to Charlie and licking her

joyfully. "Your spots!" Charlie said in amazement, as the kitten nuzzled her face. "They're glowing!"

Dappled flecks of flame seemed to ripple down Sunlight's back, and when she moved her tail, little bright sparks danced in the air.

"So that's where you got your name!" Charlie grinned. Finally it made sense.

The firekitten purred happily then she turned and padded away into the duct, her spots reflected in the steel walls. But when she reached the next turning Sunlight stopped and looked back, giving a soft, expectant mew.

"All right, little friend," Charlie said, squeezing herself along. "I'm right behind you!"

Chapter Seven
Stampede

The air shaft took a final turn then came to an end at another metal grate. Sunlight peered through the bars, and from below Charlie could hear a chorus of soft purrs and yowls.

She shoved the grate loose and peered out into the ship's main hangar. In the centre of the room was a gigantic cage, with steel mesh sides and a heavy, barred door. From inside it, the adult firecats

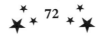

stared up at her.

Charlie also noticed that the walls of the hangar were hung with nets and traps and other kinds of hunting equipment. She shuddered. She had to stop these people.

She climbed carefully from the air duct, reaching to lift Sunlight down. As soon as her paws touched the ground, the firekitten raced excitedly towards the cage.

Sunlight put her paws on the mesh, meowing eagerly as the captured firecats padded towards her. Charlie counted ten of them inside the cage, but it was big enough to hold many more.

Then a large firecat shouldered through the pack, her spots gleaming with fierce orange light. She poked her nose through a gap in the steel mesh and Sunlight reached up to lick it fondly.

"You've found your mother!" grinned Charlie, as the glow from both creatures lit up the hangar.

"So that's why they're called firecats," a voice said, and Charlie spun round.

Taika was sitting in the shadows beneath a large, oval-shaped window. He had a gloomy, guilty look on his face.

"I never knew they could light up like that. It's really beautiful."

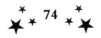

Charlie glowered at him. "You never knew because they only do it when they're happy. But you only ever saw them scared and running away. Still, I suppose they'll be worth even more now, won't they?"

Taika flushed. "Probably," he mumbled. Then he frowned. "Hang on, how did you get out of the brig?"

"You decided not to help me," Charlie said, "so I had to come up with a plan of my own."

"I'm sorry," said Taika. "There was nothing I could do."

"And what about the firecats?" Charlie asked, gesturing to the cage. "I suppose there's nothing you can do to help them either?"

Taika shook his head. "It's too late. Look."

He pointed to the window. Through

it, Charlie could see the desert plain
rushing below them at great speed. At
first she thought there was a stream
down there, then she realised she could
pick out tiny shapes. The firecats raced
madly as the *Silver Streak* soared over
their heads.

"Sunlight's pack," she said. "You've
caught up with them."

Taika nodded. "That's right. So you

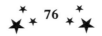

see, you're out of time."

There was a crackling sound and Charlie spotted a radio at his belt.

"Taika," his mother's voice came through. "Taika, come in. Have you got those stunners charged up?"

The boy glanced across at a series

of long metal devices hooked to the wall. Lights on their handles blinked in unison. He unhooked the radio.

"All ready down here," he said, unable to meet Charlie's eye. Then he released the talk switch.

Charlie frowned. "Why didn't you tell her I'd got out?" she asked.

Taika got slowly to his feet. "I don't know. I guess I just—"

There was a sudden excited squeak. Sunlight had noticed Taika for the first time and she ran forward, pawing happily at his ankles. He reached down and lifted her gently into his arms.

"I'm happy to see you too, Sunlight," he said, and Charlie could hear that he meant it. "I'm just... I'm really sorry for everything."

Sunlight purred softly, her spots

rippling. Through the porthole, Charlie could see the ground rushing up to meet them.

"You have to help us," she said, taking a step towards Taika. "You have to, before it's too late. Or Sunlight's going to spend the rest of her life in a cage, on some strange planet without her family to look after her. Please, Taika. You know it's the right thing to do."

The boy looked at her. There was doubt on his face, and fear. Sunlight wriggled happily in his hands. Taika bit his lip and Charlie felt a thump as the ship touched down.

Without speaking, Taika pointed to a lever on the wall. A faded sign beside it read CAGE RELEASE. Right away, Charlie knew what she had to do.

Cosmic Creatures

She reached out to grab the lever,
but before she could pull it a voice
boomed out, "Stop!"

Chapter Eight
The Pack

Major Koto charged into the hangar. "I might've known you'd find a way to escape," he growled, his face red with anger.

"I won't let you steal any more animals," Charlie shouted.

The major sneered. "There's nothing you can do, child. Those cats are *mine*."

Charlie gripped the lever.

"Don't you dare," Koto warned, starting

towards her.

But he was too slow. Charlie tugged as hard as she could and the lever clunked downwards.

For a moment all was silent. Then the barred door slid back and Charlie ducked out of the way as the firecats pounced from their cage.

The animals growled excitedly as they swarmed through the hangar. Major Koto desperately scrambled up a ladder on the wall to keep from being bowled over.

The cats streamed past him towards the open doorway, the spots in their fur gleaming joyously. Their yowls echoed in the corridor, and Charlie heard a surprised shout from one of the other rustlers.

Taika took a step back as the first firecat came bounding up to him and planted her huge paws on his jacket. The

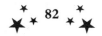

boy nodded quickly and placed Sunlight on the floor. The mother firecat nuzzled her kitten contentedly, and Charlie grinned at Taika. Nervously, he smiled back.

Then Major Koto's radio crackled and a panicked voice came through. "Those creatures!" Taika's mother shouted. "They're loose, there's one up here on the bridge! Wait, there's two! There's more! And they're glowing! No, get off! Stop licking me!"

The major grabbed his radio. "Take off!" he demanded. "Right now. We'll round them up once we're in orbit. I'm finished with this ridiculous planet."

Charlie heard the engines firing up and felt the walls vibrate. To her horror, the ship began to rise.

"Wait, what about me?" she asked. "You said you'd take me back!"

Major Koto waved a dismissive hand. "We'll drop you off at the trading post on Acheron. I'm sure that in a month or six you'll find a ship to bring you home."

Charlie's mouth fell open. "But... But I..."

"You can't do that," Taika said. His hands were trembling at his sides. "Charlie's got a family. They won't know what's happened to her!"

"She should've thought of that before she meddled in our affairs," Koto snapped. "My decision is final. We're going to cut our losses and get out of here before—"

The *Silver Streak* lurched steeply. Charlie staggered as the floor tipped. She could hear the engines complaining.

Sunlight meowed as her mother was thrown off balance, skidding across the smooth metal floor. Charlie scooped up the firekitten and held her tight.

Cosmic Creatures

Then Taika let out a gasp. A black
shape shot past the window, trailing fire
and sparks. Charlie felt her heart lift.
The hull was dented and the engine
billowed smoke, but still she recognised
the winged outline of the *Star Eagle*.

Major Koto's radio hissed. "Rustler
ship, can you hear me?" barked a voice,
and Charlie recognised her Aunt Letitia.
"*Silver Streak*, land immediately and
release your cargo."

Koto snatched up his radio. "And just
who might you be?"

"I'm the law around these parts," Aunt
Letitia told him, and Charlie couldn't
help grinning. "So do as I say or face the
consequences."

The *Star Eagle* curved across the bow of
the rustler ship, forcing it to steer sharply
out of the way.

"We have to land," the pilot's worried

voice came through the radio. "We don't have a choice. If she reports us to the authorities, we could be in real trouble."

"Don't you dare!" Major Koto shot back, but it was too late. Through the window Charlie could see the ground rushing closer. She felt a bump as the ship touched down.

Taika ran to a panel on the wall. The words OPEN MAIN HATCH were flashing, and he hit the button. Daylight flooded in as the ramp began to lower. Hot wind howled into the hangar.

Then Charlie heard another kind of howling, and shielded her eyes. Out on the plain the firecat herd came sweeping closer, moving as one towards the ship.

From behind her, Charlie heard answering growls and the pounding of feet. The captured firecats swarmed back through the hangar, past the cage

that had once imprisoned them. Taika
beamed proudly as they rushed by, their
spots shining bright against the daylight
streaming through the open hatch.

They leapt down on to the sand and
ran to join the huge herd that came
thundering across the plain to greet

them. Charlie placed Sunlight down as the firekitten's mother picked herself up and padded towards them.

"Go," Charlie said, patting Sunlight's furry bottom. "Join your pack."

Sunlight gave a happy mew and trotted towards her mother.

But a voice said, "Not so fast!"

A hand reached down and grabbed the kitten by the scruff of her neck.

Major Koto dangled Sunlight in front of his face, grinning greedily. "I think I'll keep this one," he said. "Should fetch enough to pay for the trip, and maybe a bit more."

Sunlight's mother growled but Major Koto kept hold of the firekitten, backing towards the door. The big firecat watched cautiously, unsure what to do.

"Put her down!" Charlie shouted. "You can't have her."

Koto's eyes flashed. "Get off my ship," he barked. Then he glanced over at Taika. "You as well. I don't want to see your faces ever again."

Sunlight wriggled and yowled, but Koto's grip was too strong. He reached the door, backed through it and reached for the switch marked CLOSE.

"She's mine," he hissed. "And there's absolutely nothing you can— What's happening?"

He looked down in surprise and Charlie gasped as she saw the major's feet leaving the floor. He cried out, tipping sideways.

Suddenly Charlie realised there was a glowing energy field around him, extending from the corridor at his back. The major rolled over until he was almost upside down. His legs kicked helplessly. Sunlight slipped from his grasp, floating in the air and waving her paws.

Then a dark shape drifted into the light of the doorway and Charlie grinned.

"Random!"

The robot floated closer, his power cable trailing behind him. "Hello, everyone," he said. "I've just woken up. What did I miss?"

Major Koto hung in mid-air, turning slowly. He cursed and waved his arms as he tried to get his feet back on the ground.

"Put me down!" he shouted. "That's an order."

Charlie laughed. "I don't think we'll be taking any more orders from you," she said. Then she remembered something, and turned to Random.

"Hold on," she said. "I thought you couldn't lift heavy objects?"

The robot nodded. "Oh, I can lift them," he said. "Just not for very long."

And with that the force field around
Major Koto broke and he crashed to the
floor. Sunlight landed neatly on his chest,
then she ran up to lick the major's face.
He lay on the metal floor and groaned.

Charlie carried the rescued firekitten

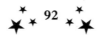

down the *Silver Streak*'s ramp with
Random and Taika at her side. Ahead of
them padded Sunlight's mother, purring
happily as she saw the rest of her pack
spread out across the plain.

Major Koto trudged down with the rest
of his crew, looking around nervously. The
Star Eagle had landed a short distance
away and Aunt Letitia was striding
towards them, followed closely by Maki.

"I hope you know that what you're
doing is illegal," Aunt Letitia snapped,
before Koto had a chance to speak.
"I could lock you all up and call the
interstellar authorities. Instead, I've
decided to give you a choice."

Major Koto snarled. "What choice?"

Aunt Letitia smiled thinly. "Well, you
can leave this planet right now and never,
ever come back."

"Or?" the major demanded. "What's the

other option?"

Aunt Letitia glanced at Taika and her face softened. "Or you can stay," she said. "Stay on Vela and help build our new colony."

The major barked a laugh. "Stay here? At the back end of the universe? I don't think so. I'll take option A, thank you very much. The sooner I'm off this planet, the better."

And he marched back up the ramp, his boots clumping on the steel.

Most of his crew followed but Taika held back. His mother paused halfway up the ramp and beckoned to her son.

"Come on, love," she said gently. "I'll make your favourite supper."

But Taika didn't move. He looked from his mother to Charlie, then to Aunt Letitia. "Do you mean it?" he asked her. "About staying to help?"

Aunt Letitia nodded seriously. "We can always find a use for a strong boy like you," she said. "And a strong woman too," she added, glancing at Taika's mother. "Life in Firecat Plains isn't easy, but

there's always work to be done. And we have a school, and a theatre, and you can visit Charlie in the holidays."

Taika bit his lip and Charlie saw hope in his eyes. He clasped his hands together as he turned to his mother.

"Couldn't we, Mum?" he asked. "Couldn't we stay? You know, I've been thinking about it a lot, and I don't think this is a very good life. Flying around the galaxy and stealing wild animals? It's not... Well, it's not right."

Taika's mother frowned. "I thought you liked the adventure. All those different worlds, different creatures."

Taika nodded. "I like the animal part. Finding them, and looking after them. I just don't like having to sell them."

"You know, we have a farm in Firecat Plains," Aunt Letitia said. "Horses, desert ox, mooncalves. I could get you a job there, if you like. When you're not at school, of course."

Taika's eyes widened. "That'd be amazing," he breathed. Then he looked pleadingly at his mother. "Don't you think it'd be good for us to have a real home for a change? A real home, and real friends?"

He glanced at Charlie and she gave him an encouraging smile.

The pilot considered her son's words, then, slowly, she nodded.

"Maybe," she said, stepping down from the ramp. "If it's what you want, we could give it a try."

Maki let out a whoop and Aunt Letitia beamed, putting a friendly arm around Taika's mother's shoulders. "You won't regret it," she said. "I promise."

Charlie turned to Maki. "You fixed the ship," she said, gesturing to the *Star Eagle*.

"Nice work."

Her brother blushed. "Aunt Letitia repaired the engines," he admitted. "I just helped to get the main computer back online."

"Well, you got here just in time," Charlie told him. "I almost got kidnapped too, just like the firecats!"

She placed Sunlight down on the sand, crouching to ruffle the firekitten's soft blue fur. Taika joined them, giving the kitten a friendly pat.

"Be careful with that paw," he said as Sunlight licked his fingers.

Charlie gave the kitten one last fond scratch behind the ears. "I'm sad to see you go," she said. "But I know it's the best thing. And who knows, maybe we'll see you again next year!"

The firekitten purred and gave Charlie's fingers a final lick. Then she bounded away, hurrying towards her mother. Out on the plain the rest of the firecat herd were waiting patiently for their last two members to join them.

At last the pack started off, the dust clouds rising as their paws drummed the desert ground. As they gathered speed they turned in a sweeping circle around the two spaceships, and for a moment Charlie felt as though she was in the eye of a great hurricane, a vortex of swirling dust and moving bodies.

Then the cats let out a cry and their spots lit up in unison, gleaming like lava

amid the rising clouds. Sparks rose and
the dust itself seemed to glow. Charlie
laughed out loud. She'd never seen
anything so beautiful.

Then the pack turned away and
continued their journey across the
plain. For a moment, Charlie saw
Sunlight running gleefully beside her

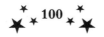

mother, the spots gleaming in her fur.
Then she vanished from Charlie's sight.

"I'm going to miss her," she said to
Random. "I almost wish we could've
taken her home with us."

"She is a wild creature," the robot
said. "She belongs with her family."

"I know," Charlie said. Then she

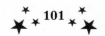

grinned. "Hey, I wonder what other amazing animals we might come across out here? The holiday's only just started, after all!"

Look out for another adventure
with Charlie and Random:

The Runaway Rumblebear

ILLUSTRATED BY
**SOPHY
WILLIAMS**

TOM HUDDLESTON

Chapter One
The Vanishing Apples

Charlie looked up at the tall white tree.
Its top branches were bowed down with
sparkly blue shimmer-apples.

"Come on, Random," she called out.
"Let's get picking!"

But Random the robot wasn't paying
any attention.

His ball-shaped body floated above the
ground. His metal arms were stretched
out wide and his silver eyes flashed with

concentration.
His hands twirled
as five shimmer-apples bounced
between them.

Charlie grinned. "That's very clever,"
she said. "But we're here to pick the
apples, Random. Not juggle them."

Random tried to stop juggling, but the
apples were flying too fast for him. His
arms began to whir madly and his body
spun like a top.

Finally the apples went flying and
splatted to the ground.